GOOD WORK, SECRET SEVEN

GOOD WORK, SECRET SEVEN

by
ENID BLYTON

Illustrated by
BRUNO KAY

Hodder
Children's
Books

a division of Hodder Headline plc

Copyright © Enid Blyton Ltd.

Enid Blyton's signature is a Registered Trade Mark of Enid Blyton Ltd.

First published in Great Britain in 1954
by Hodder and Stoughton
Revised edition 1992
This hardback edition published 1997

ISBN 0-340-70395-4

Typeset by Hewer Text Composition Services, Edinburgh
Printed and bound in Great Britain
by Clays Ltd, St Ives plc

Hodder Children's Books
a division of Hodder Headline plc
338 Euston Road
London NW1 3BH

CONTENTS

It is illegal for fireworks to be sold to children. We recommend that fireworks should always be stored and handled by adults.

Always follow the Firework Safety Code:

1. Keep fireworks in a closed box. Take them out one at a time and put the lid back at once.
2. Follow the instructions on each firework carefully. Read them by torchlight – never a naked flame.
3. Keep pets indoors.
4. Light fireworks at arm's length – preferably with a safety firework lighter or fuse wick.
5. Stand well back.
6. Never go back to a firework once lit – it may go off in your face.
7. Never throw fireworks.
8. Never put fireworks in pockets.
9. Never fool with fireworks.
10. Site the bonfire away from the house, garage or shed.
11. Light the bonfire with firelighters – not paraffin or petrol.
12. Keep a bucket or two of water handy just in case.
13. Pour water on bonfire embers before going indoors.

CHAPTER ONE

Secret Seven meeting

'WHEN ARE the Secret Seven going to have their next meeting?' said Susie to her brother Jack.

'That's nothing to do with *you*!' said Jack. 'You don't belong to it, and what's more, you never will!'

'Goodness! *I* don't want to belong to it!' said Susie, putting on a very surprised voice. 'If I want to belong to a secret society I can always get one of my own. I did once before, and it was a better one than yours.'

'Don't be silly,' said Jack. 'Our Secret Seven is the best in the world. Why, just think of the things we've done and the adventures we've had! I bet we'll have another one soon.'

'I bet you won't,' said Susie, annoyingly.

'You've been meeting in that shed at the bottom of Peter and Janet's garden for weeks now, and there isn't even the *smell* of a mystery!'

'Well, mysteries don't grow on trees, nor do adventures,' said Jack. 'They just happen all in a minute. Anyway, I'm not going to talk about the Secret Seven any more, and you needn't think you'll get anything out of me, because you won't, Susie. And please go out of my room and let me get on with this book.'

'I know your latest password,' said Susie, halfway through the door.

'You do *not*!' said Jack, quite fiercely. 'I haven't mentioned it, and I haven't even written it down so that I won't forget it. You're a story-teller, Susie.'

'I'm not! I'm just telling you so as to warn you to choose a *new* password!' said Susie, and slid out of the door.

Jack stared after her. What an *annoying* sister she was! *Did* she know the password? No, she *couldn't* know it, possibly!

It was true what Susie had said. The Secret Seven had been meeting for weeks, and absolutely nothing had turned up. Certainly the seven had plenty of fun together, but after having so many exciting adventures it was a bit dull just to go on playing games and talking.

Jack looked in his notebook. When was the next meeting? Tomorrow night, in Peter's shed. Well, that would be quite exciting, because all the members had been told to bring any old clothes they could find. They were going to make the Guy for their bonfire at the next meeting. It would be fun seeing what everyone had brought.

Bonfire night was next week. Jack got up and rummaged in one of his drawers. Ah, there was his money which he kept in an old tin. Jack counted it carefully. There was just enough to buy a firework called a Humdinger. Jack was sure none of the other members of the Secret Seven would have one of those.

'Fizzzzz – whoooosh – '

'Jack! What in the world are you doing? Are you ill?' called an anxious voice, and his mother's head came round the door.

'No, Mother, I'm all right,' said Jack. 'I was thinking of a Humdinger on Bonfire Night and the noise it will make.'

'Humdinger? Whatever's that?' asked his mother.

'It's a big firework that makes lots of bangs and whooshes. I've saved up enough money to get one. Please will you ask Daddy to buy me one when he goes to do the shopping for Bonfire Night?'

'Give your father the money and he'll get

you one,' said his mother. 'Oh, Jack, how untidy your bedroom is. Do tidy it up!'

'I was *just* tidying it, Mother,' said Jack. 'Hey, could you let me have some of those chocolate biscuits out of the tin, Mother? We're having a Secret Seven meeting tomorrow night.'

'Very well. Take seven,' said his mother.

'Eight, you mean,' called Jack, as she went out of the room. '*Mother*! Eight, I want. You've forgotten Scamper.'

'Goodness! Well, if you *must* waste good chocolate biscuits on a dog, take eight,' called his mother.

Good, thought Jack. We've all got to take something nice to eat tomorrow night, for the meeting. Choc biscuits will be fine! Now, what was the password? Guy Fawkes, wasn't it? Or was that last time's? No, that's the one. Guy Fawkes – and a jolly good password, seeing that Bonfire Night is soon coming! Why does Susie say she knows it? She doesn't!

The meeting was for half-past five, in Peter's shed, and all the Secret Seven meant to be there. Just before the half-hour five children began to file in at Peter's gate and make their way down the garden to the shed where the meetings were held.

The shed door was shut, but a light shone

from inside. On the door were the letters S.S., put there by Peter. It was dark, and one by one torches shone on the door as the members arrived.

Rat-tat!

'Password, please!' That was Peter's voice inside.

'Guy Fawkes!' answered the members one by one.

Pamela was first. Then came Jack, hurrying in case he was late. Then George, carrying a bag of rosy apples as his share of the food.

Then Barbara, wondering if the password was Guy Fawkes or Bonfire Night. Oh dear!

Rat-tat! She knocked at the door.

'Password!'

'Er – Bonfire Night,' said Barbara.

The door remained shut, and there was a dead silence inside. Barbara gave a little giggle.

'All right. I know it! Guy Fawkes!'

The door opened and she went in. Everyone was there except Colin.

'He's late,' said Peter. 'Bother him! Look, what a spread we've got tonight!'

The shed was warm and cosy inside. It was lit by two candles, and there was a small oil-stove at the back. On a table made of a box was spread the food the members had brought.

'Apples. Ginger buns. Doughnuts. Peppermint rock, and what's in this bag? Oh yes, hazelnuts from your garden, Pam. *And* you've remembered to bring nutcrackers too. Good. And I've brought orangeade. What a feast!' said Peter.

'I wish Colin would hurry up,' said Janet. 'Oh, here he is!'

There was the sound of running feet and somebody banged at the door. Rat-tat!

'Password!' yelled everyone.

'Guy Fawkes!' answered a voice, and Peter opened the door.

Well, would you believe it! It was *Susie* outside, grinning all over her cheeky face. *Susie*!

CHAPTER TWO

That awful Susie!

'SUSIE!' CRIED Jack, springing up in a rage. 'How dare you! You – you – you . . .'

He caught hold of his sister and held her tight. She laughed at him.

'It's all right; I just wanted to give your high-and-mighty members a shock. Aha! I know your password, see?'

'How did you know it?' demanded Peter. 'Let her go, Jack. We'll turn her out in a minute. How did you know the password, Susie?'

'I got it from Jack, of course,' said Susie, most surprisingly.

Everyone stared at poor Jack, who went as red as a beetroot. He glared at Susie.

'You're a wicked story-teller! I never told you the password and I didn't even write it down, in case you found it. How *did* you know it? Were you listening in the bushes round the shed? Did you hear us say the password as we came in?'

'No. If I had, Scamper would have barked,' said Susie, which was quite true. 'I tell you, Jack, I heard you say it yourself. You were talking in your sleep last night and you kept yelling out "Guy Fawkes! Let me in! Guy Fawkes!" So I guessed you were trying to get

into the meeting in your sleep and were yelling out the password.'

Jack groaned. 'I do talk in my sleep, but who would have thought I'd yell out the password? I'll keep my bedroom door shut in future. I'm sorry, Peter. What are we going to do with Susie? She ought to be punished for bursting in on our secret meeting like this!'

'Well, we've nothing important to discuss, so we'll make Susie sit in that corner over there, and we'll have our feast, and not offer her a single thing,' said Peter, firmly. 'I'm tired of

Susie, always trying to upset our Society. Pam and Barbara, sit her down over there.'

Everyone was so very cross with Susie that she began to feel upset. 'It was only a joke,' she said. 'Anyway, your meetings are silly. You go on and on having them and nothing happens at all. Let me go.'

'Well, promise on your honour you'll never try to trick us again or upset our meetings?' said Peter, sternly.

'No. I won't promise,' said Susie. 'And I shan't sit still in this corner, and I shan't keep quiet. You're to let me go.'

'Certainly not,' began Peter. 'You forced yourself in, and you can jolly well stop and see us eating all . . .'

He stopped very suddenly as he heard the sound of panting breath, and running feet coming down the garden path.

'It's Colin!' said Janet.

There was a loud rat-tat at the door, and the password. 'Guy Fawkes! Quick, open the door.'

The door was opened and Colin came in, blinking at the sudden light, after the darkness outside.

THAT AWFUL SUSIE!

'Hey, I've had an adventure! It might be something for the Secret Seven. Listen!'

'Wait! Turn Susie out first!' said Peter.

Colin stared in surprise at seeing Susie there. She gave a sudden giggle, and Jack scowled at her.

'What's she doing here, anyway?' asked Colin, most astonished, as he watched Susie being hustled out of the shed.

The door was slammed and locked. Scamper, the golden spaniel who belonged to Peter and Janet, barked loudly. He hadn't at all approved of Susie being in his shed. He knew she wasn't a member!

'Tell you about Susie later,' said Peter. 'Now, Colin, what's all this about? Why are you late, and what's happened? And for goodness' sake, let's all talk quietly, because Susie is sure to be listening at the door!'

'I'll jolly well see that she isn't,' said Jack, getting up, but Peter pulled him back.

'Sit down! Don't you know it's just what Susie would like, to be chased all over the garden in the dark, spoiling our feast and our meeting and everything! Let her listen at

13

the door if she wants to. She won't hear a word if we whisper. Be quiet, Scamper! I can't hear myself speak with you barking at the top of your voice. Can't *you* whisper too?'

Scamper couldn't. He stopped barking and lay down with his back to Peter, looking rather hurt. But he soon turned himself round again when Colin began his tale.

'I was coming along to the meeting, shining my torch as I came, and when I got to the corner of Beeches Lane, I heard somebody in the clump of bushes there. You know there's quite a little thicket at that corner. There was a lot of whispering going on, and then suddenly I heard a yell and a groan . . .'

'Gosh!' said Janet, startled.

'And somebody fell heavily. I shone my torch at the bushes, but someone knocked it out of my hand,' went on Colin. 'Then I heard the sound of running feet. I went to pick up my torch, which was still shining brightly on the ground, but by the time I shone it into the bushes again, nobody was there!'

'You were really brave to pick it up and look into the bushes,' said Peter. 'What was going on, do you think?'

'I can't imagine, except that there was a quarrel of some sort,' said Colin. 'That isn't all, though. Look what I found in the bushes.'

The Secret Seven were now so excited that they had quite forgotten about whispering. They had raised their voices, and not one of them remembered that Susie might be outside. Scamper gave a little warning growl, but nobody paid any attention.

Colin was holding out a worn and battered notebook, with an elastic band round it. 'I've had a quick look inside,' he said, 'and it might be important. A lot of it is in code, I can't read it, and there's a lot of nonsense too. At least it

sounds like nonsense, but I expect it's part of a code. Look!'

They all looked. Everyone began to feel excited. Peter turned the pages and came to a list written down one page. 'Look!' he said. 'Here's a list that might be a record of stolen goods. Listen . . . silver candlesticks, three-branches, cigarette box with initials A.G.B., four silver cups, engraved . . .'

Jack sprang up. 'I know what all that is! My father read the list out at breakfast this morn-ing. It was in the paper. It's a list of the things stolen from the famous cricketer, Bedwall, last night. Whew! Do you suppose we're on to something, Peter?'

CHAPTER THREE

Exciting plans

THE SECRET Seven were so thrilled that their excitement made Scamper begin to bark again. He just couldn't help it when he heard them all talking at once. He waved his plumy tail and pawed at Peter, who took no notice at all.

'It must be a notebook kept by one of the thieves, a list of things he stole!'

'What else does it say? I wish we could understand all this stuff in secret code. Wait, look, here's a note scribbled right across this page! See what it says?'

'"Gang meet in old workmen's shed, back of Lane's garage,"' read Peter. '"5 p.m. Wednesday." Whew! That's tomorrow. Gosh, we *are* on to something.'

EXCITING PLANS

Everyone began to talk excitedly again, and Scamper thought it was a very good time to sample a chocolate biscuit and perhaps a ginger bun. Before he did so he ran to the door and sniffed.

Yes. Susie was outside. Scamper could smell her. He growled a little, but as no one took any notice, and he was afraid to bark again, he went back to the good things on the little box-table.

'What are we going to do about this? Tell the police?' asked Colin, who felt most important at bringing all this exciting news to the Seven.

'No. I'll tell you what we'll do,' said Peter. 'We'll creep round to that old shed tomorrow night ourselves, and as soon as we see the gang is safely there, one of us can rush round to the police-station, while the rest keep guard on the shed.'

It was decided that that would be a good sensible and exciting thing to do. Pam gave a huge sigh.

'Excitement makes me feel so hungry. Can't we start on the buns and things? Oh, Scamper, you've been helping yourself! Thief-dog!'

'Scamper! Have you really been taking things?' said Peter, shocked. 'Go into the corner.'

'He's only taken a choc biscuit and a ginger bun,' said Jack, counting everything quickly. 'There should be eight of each thing, but there are only seven of the biscuits and the buns. So really he's only eaten what we brought for *him*, the eighth person.'

'Well, he shouldn't begin before we do,' said Peter. 'He ought to know his manners. Corner, Scamper!'

Poor Scamper retired to the corner, licking his lips for stray chocolate crumbs. He looked so woe-begone that everyone felt extremely sorry for him.

The clothes brought by the Secret Seven for the Guy were quite forgotten. The evening's events were much too exciting even to think about the Guy. The Seven made their plans as they ate.

'Gosh, we forgot all about Susie!' said Peter, suddenly. 'We've been yelling out our plans at the tops of our voices. Bother! Scamper, see if Susie is at the door!'

Scamper obediently ran to the door and sniffed. No, Susie was no longer there. He came back and sat down by Peter, putting his lovely golden head on the boy's knee, hoping for a forgiving pat.

'Oh, so she's not there. You'd have growled if she had been, wouldn't you, Scamper?' said

Peter, stroking the dog's silky head and fondling his long ears. 'Well, Susie will be most astonished to hear about our adventure when it's over – serve her right for laughing at us and trying to spoil our meeting!'

It was arranged that all the Seven should go quietly to Lane's garage the next night, after tea. Colin knew Larry, a boy who helped at the garage, and it would be quite easy for the Seven to talk to him and admire the cars until it was time to look about for the workmen's shed behind the garage. Then what would happen? A little thrill of excitement ran all the way up Peter's back when he thought of it.

The Secret Seven are on the move again! he thought. What a good thing, after all these dull weeks when nothing happened!

It seemed a long time till the next afternoon. Everyone at the schools the Secret Seven went to was sure that something was up. The Seven wore their badges, and a lot of whispering went on. All the members looked important and serious.

Susie was very annoying. She kept looking at Pam, Janet and Barbara, who were in her class, and giggling. Whenever she passed them she whispered in their ear:

'Guy Fawkes! Guy Fawkes!'

This was very annoying because it was still the password of the Secret Seven! They had completely forgotten to change it the night before, in the excitement of making plans. Now Susie still knew it. They must change it as quickly as they could.

At four o'clock all the Secret Seven rushed home early to tea, so that they could be off again immediately to the garage. They were to meet Colin there at a quarter to five.

All their mothers were astonished to see how quickly the children gobbled their teas that afternoon, but luckily nobody was made to stop at home afterwards. One by one they made their way to the garage. Scamper was left behind, in case he barked at an awkward moment.

Everyone was at the garage at a quarter to five. Only fifteen minutes more! Now, where was Larry? They must talk to him for a little while, and then creep round to the shed at the back. How exciting!

CHAPTER FOUR

A dreadful shock

COLIN WAS already looking for Larry, the boy he knew who helped at the garage. Ah, there he was, washing a car over in the corner. Colin went over to him, and the other six followed.

'Good evening,' said Larry, grinning at the Seven. He had a shock of fair hair and a very dirty face and twinkling eyes. 'Come to help me?'

'I wish we were allowed to,' said Colin. 'I'd love to mess about with cars. Larry, can we have a look at the ones you've got in the garage now?'

'Yes, so long as you don't open the doors,' said the lad, splashing the water very near Colin's feet.

The Seven divided up and went to look at the

cars near the doorway and wide windows, so that they could keep an eye on anyone passing. They might see the 'gang', whoever they were.

'Look! Doesn't *he* look as if he might be one of the gang?' whispered Barbara, nudging Jack as a man went by.

Jack glanced at him.

'Idiot!' he said. 'That's my headmaster. Good thing he didn't hear you! Still, he does look a bit grim!'

'It's five to five,' said George in a low voice. 'I think we'd better go round to the shed soon, Peter.'

'Not yet,' said Peter. 'We don't want to be there when the men arrive. Seen anyone likely to belong to the gang?'

'Not really,' said George. 'Everybody looks rather *ordinary*. But then, the gang might look ordinary too. Gosh, I *am* beginning to feel excited!'

A little later, when the garage clock said a minute past five, Peter gave the signal to move. They all said goodbye to Larry, who playfully splashed hose-water round their ankles as they ran out.

'Bother him, my socks are soaked,' said Jack. 'Do we go down this alley-way, Peter?'

'Yes. I'll go first, and if all's clear I'll give a low whistle,' said Peter.

He went down the alley in the darkness, holding his torch, but not putting it on. He came to the yard behind the garage, where the workmen's shed was.

He stopped in delight. There was a light in it! The gang *were* in there, then! My word, if only they could catch the whole lot at once.

Peter gave a low whistle, and the others

trooped down the alley to him. They all wore rubber-soled shoes, and made no noise at all. Their hearts beat fast and Barbara felt out of breath, hers thumped so hard. They all stared at the little shed, with the dim light shining from its one small window.

'They must be there,' whispered Jack. 'Let's creep up and see if we can peep in at the window.'

They crept noiselessly up to the shed. The window was high up and Peter had to put a few bricks on top of one another to stand on, so that he could reach the window.

He stepped down and whispered to the others: 'They're there. I can't see them, but I can hear them. Shall we get the police straight away, do you think?'

'Well, I'd like to be sure it isn't just *workmen* inside,' said Jack. 'They might be having their tea there or something, you know. Workmen do have a lot of meals, and that shed's pretty cosy, I should think.'

'What are we to do, then? We can't knock on the door and say, "Are you workmen or do you belong to the gang?"' said Peter.

A loud bang came suddenly from the shed and made everyone jump. Barbara clutched at George and made him jump again.

'Was that a gun?' she said. 'They're not shooting, are they?'

'*Don't* grab me like that!' said George, in a fierce whisper. 'You nearly made me yell out. How do I know if it's shooting?'

Another loud bang came, and the Seven once more jumped violently, Peter was puzzled. What was happening in that shed? He suddenly saw that there was a keyhole. Perhaps if he bent down and looked through that he would be able to see what was happening inside.

So he bent down and squinted through the keyhole, and sure enough, he got quite a view, though a narrow one, of the inside of the candle-lit shed.

What he saw filled him with such astonishment that he let out a loud exclamation. He couldn't believe his eyes. He simply couldn't!

'What is it, what is it?' cried Pam, quite forgetting to speak in a whisper. 'Are they shooting? Let *me* look!'

She dragged Peter away and put her eye to the keyhole, and she, too, gave a squeal. Then, to the amazement of all the others but Peter, she began to kick and bang at the locked door! She shouted loudly:

'It's *Susie* in there, Susie and some others! I can see her grinning like anything, and they've got big paper bags to pop. That's what made the bangs. It's Susie; it's all a trick; it's SUSIE!'

So it was. Susie, with Jim and Doris and Ronnie, and now they were rolling over the floor, squealing with laughter. Oh, what a *wonderful* trick they had played on the Secret Seven!

CHAPTER FIVE

A victory for Susie

THE SECRET Seven were so angry that they hardly knew what to do. So it was Susie and her friends who had planned all this! While Susie had been boldly giving the password and forcing her way into their meeting the night before, her friends were pretending to scuffle in the bushes to stop Colin and make him think something really serious was going on!

'They took me in properly,' groaned Colin. 'I really thought it was men scuffling there, and I was so pleased to find that notebook when they had run off! It was too dark to spot that they weren't men, of course.'

'No wonder Susie giggled all the time she was in our shed, and laughed when Colin

30

rushed in to tell us of his adventure!' said Janet. 'Horrid, tiresome girl!'

'She's the worst sister possible,' said Jack, gloomily. 'Fancy putting that list of stolen things in the notebook, of course, *she* had heard my father read them out at breakfast-time too. Bother Susie!'

George kicked at the shed door. From the inside came the sound of shrieks of delighted laughter, and some enormous guffaws from Jim, who, like Doris, was rolling about from side to side, holding his aching sides. Oh, what

a joke! Oh, to think they had brought the stuck-up Secret Seven all the way to this shed, just to see *them*!

'You just wait till you unlock the door and come out!' called Jack. 'You just wait! I'll pull your hair till you squeal, Susie. I'm ashamed of you!'

More squeals of laughter, and a loud, 'Ho, ho, ho,' from Jim again. It really was maddening.

'There's seven of us, and only four of you,' cried Colin, warningly. 'And we'll wait here till you come out, see? You hadn't thought of that, had you?'

'Oh yes, we had,' called Susie. 'But you'll let us go free – you see if you don't.'

'We shan't!' said Jack, furiously. 'Unlock the door.'

'Listen, Jack,' said Susie. 'This is going to be a LOVELY tale to tell all the others at school. Won't the Secret Seven be laughed at? Silly old Secret Seven, tricked by a stupid notebook. They think themselves so grand and so clever, but they're sure that four children in a shed are a gang of robbers shooting at one another! And we only had paper bags to pop!'

The four inside popped paper bags again and roared with laughter. The Secret Seven felt gloomier and gloomier.

'You know, Susie will make everyone roar with laughter about this,' said Colin. 'We shan't be able to hold our heads up for ages. Susie's right. We'll have to let them go free, and not set on them when they come out.'

'No!' said Peter and Jack.

'*Yes*,' said Colin. 'We'll *have* to make a bargain with them, and Susie jolly well knows it. We'll have to let them go free in return for their keeping silent about this. It's no good, we've got to. *I* don't want all the silly kids in the first form roaring with laughter and popping paper bags at me whenever I go by. And they will. I know them!'

There was a silence. It dawned on everyone that Colin was right. Susie had got the best of them. They *couldn't* allow anyone to make a laughing-stock of their Secret Seven Society. They were so proud of it; it was the best Secret Society in the world.

Peter sighed. Susie *was* a pest. Somehow they must pay her back for this tiresome, aggravating trick. But for the moment she had won.

'Susie! You win, for the present!' said Peter. 'You can go free, and we won't even pull your hair, if you promise solemnly not to say a single word about this to anyone at school.'

'All right,' called Susie, triumphantly. 'I knew you'd have to make that bargain. What a swizz for you! Silly old Secret Seven! Meeting solemnly week after week with never a thing to do! Well, we're coming out, so mind you keep your word.'

The door was unlocked from inside and the four came out, laughing and grinning. They stalked through the Secret Seven, noses in the air, enjoying their triumph. Jack's fingers

itched to grab at Susie's hair, but he kept them in his pockets.

'Goodbye. Thanks for a marvellous show,' said the irritating Susie. 'Let us know when you want another adventure, and we'll provide one for you. See you later, Jack!'

They went off down the alley-way, still laughing. It was a gloomy few minutes for the Seven, as they stood in the dark yard, hearing the footsteps going down the alley.

'We MUST find something really exciting ourselves now, as soon as possible,' said Colin. 'That will stop Susie and the others jeering at us.'

'If only we could!' said Peter. 'But the more you look for an adventure the farther away it seems. Bother Susie! What a horrible evening we've had!'

But it wasn't quite the end of it. A lamp suddenly shone out nearby and a voice said:

'Now then! What are you doing here? Clear off, you kids, or I'll report you to your parents!'

It was the policeman! Well! To think they had been turned off by the police as if *they* were a gang of robbers, and they had had such high hopes of fetching this very policeman to capture a gang in that shed! It was all very, very sad.

In deep silence the Seven left the yard and went gloomily up the alley-way. They could hardly say goodnight to one another. Oh, for a real adventure, one that would make them important again, and fill their days with breathless excitement!

Be patient, Secret Seven. One may be just round the corner. You just never know!

CHAPTER SIX

A sudden adventure

NEXT DAY Peter and Janet talked and talked about Susie's clever trick. Why, oh why, had they allowed themselves to be so easily taken in? Scamper listened sympathetically to their gloomy voices, and went first to one, then to the other, wagging his tail.

'He's trying to tell us he's sorry about it!' said Janet, with a little laugh. 'Oh, Scamper, if only we'd taken you with us, you'd have known Susie was in that shed with her silly friends, and somehow you'd have found a way of telling us.'

Scamper gave a little whine, and then lay on his back, his legs working hard, as if he were pedalling a bicycle upside down. He always did this when he wanted to make the two children laugh.

They laughed now, and patted him. Good old Scamper!

Their mother popped her head in at the door. 'Don't forget you're to go to tea with old Mrs Penton this afternoon.'

'My bike's got a puncture, Mummy,' said Janet. 'It's *such* a long way to walk. Need I go?'

'Well, Daddy is going out in the car this

afternoon. He can take you there, and fetch you back afterwards,' said Mummy. 'He'll call for you about six o'clock, so mind you don't keep him waiting.'

The car was waiting outside Janet's school for her that afternoon, with Daddy at the wheel. They picked Peter up at his school gates, and Daddy drove them to Mrs Penton's. She had been their mother's old nanny, and she was very fond of them.

They forgot all about their annoyance with Susie when they saw the magnificent tea that Mrs Penton had got ready.

'Goodness – cream buns! How delicious!'

said Janet. 'And chocolate éclairs. Did Mummy like them when you were her nanny?'

'Oh yes, she ate far too many once, and I was up all night with her,' said Mrs Penton. 'Very naughty she was, that day, just wouldn't do what she was told, and finished up by overeating. Dear, dear, what a night I had with her!'

It seemed impossible that their mother could ever have been naughty or have eaten too many cream buns and éclairs. Still, it would be a very easy thing to eat at least a dozen of them, Janet thought, looking at the lovely puffy cream oozing out of the big buns, and those éclairs! She felt very kindly towards the little girl who was now grown-up, and her own mother!

They played the big musical box after tea, and looked at Mrs Penton's funny old picture-books. Then the clock suddenly struck six.

'Gosh, Daddy said we were to be ready at six!' said Peter, jumping up. 'Hurry up, Janet. Thank you very much, Mrs Penton, for such a smashing tea.'

Hoot – hoo – ! That was Daddy already outside waiting for them. Mrs Penton kissed them both.

'Thank you very, very much,' said Janet. 'I *have* enjoyed myself!'

They ran down the path and climbed into the car at the back. It was quite dark, and Daddy's headlights shed broad beams over the road.

'Good children,' he said. 'I only had to wait half a minute.' He put in the clutch and pressed down the accelerator; the car slid off down the road.

'I've just got to call at the station for some parcels,' said Daddy. 'I'll leave the car in the yard with you in it. I shan't be a minute.'

They came to the station, and Daddy backed the car out of the way at one end of the station yard. He jumped out and disappeared into the lit entrance of the station.

Peter and Janet lay back on the seat, beginning to feel that they *might* have over-eaten! Janet felt sleepy and shut her eyes. Peter began to think about the evening before, and Susie's clever trick.

He suddenly heard hurried footsteps, and thought it must be his father back again. The door was quickly opened and a man got in. Then the opposite door was opened and another man sat down in the seat beside the driver's.

Peter thought his father had brought a friend with him to give him a lift, and he wondered who it was. It was dark in the station yard, and he couldn't see the other man's face at all. Then the headlights went on, and the car moved quickly out of the yard.

Peter got a really terrible shock as soon as the car passed a lamppost. The man driving the car wasn't his father! It was somebody he didn't know at all, a man with a low-brimmed

hat, and rather long hair down to his collar. Peter's father never had long hair. Whoever was this driving the car?

The boy sat quite still. He looked at the other man when they went by a lamppost again. No, that wasn't his father either! It was a man he had never seen before. His head was bare and the hair was very short, quite different from his companion's.

A little cold feeling crept round Peter's heart. Who were these men? Were they stealing his father's car? What was he to do?

Janet stirred a little. Peter leaned over to her and put his lips right to her ear.

'Janet!' he whispered. 'Are you awake? Listen to me. I think Daddy's car is being stolen by two men, and they don't know we're at the back. Slip quietly down to the floor, so that if they happen to turn round they won't see us. Quick now, for goodness' sake!'

CHAPTER SEVEN

Something to work on

JANET WAS awake now, very much awake! She took one scared look at the heads of the two men in front, suddenly outlined by a street lamp, and slid quickly down to the floor. She began to tremble.

Peter slipped down beside her. 'Don't be frightened. I'll look after you. So long as the men don't know we're here, we're all right.'

'But where are they taking us?' whispered Janet, glad that the rattling of the car drowned her voice.

'I've no idea. They've gone down the main street, and now they're in a part of the town I don't know,' whispered Peter. 'Hallo, they're stopping. Keep down, Janet, and don't make a sound!'

The driver stopped the car and peered out of the open window. 'You're all right here,' he said to his companion. 'No one's about. Get in touch with Q8061 at once. Tell him Sid's place, five o'clock any evening. I'll be there.'

'Right,' said the other man and opened his door cautiously. Then he shut it again, and ducked his head down.

'What's up? Someone coming?' said the driver.

'No. I think I've dropped something,' said the other man, in a muffled voice. He appeared to be groping over the floor. 'I'm sure I heard something drop.'

'For goodness' sake! Clear out now while the going's good!' said the driver impatiently. 'The police will be on the look-out for this car in a few minutes. I'm going to Sid's, and I don't know anything at all about you, see? Not a thing!'

The other man muttered something and opened his door again. He slid out into the dark road. The driver got out on his side; both doors were left open, as the men did not want to make the slightest noise that might call attention to them.

Peter sat up cautiously. He could not see or hear anything of the two men. The darkness had swallowed them completely. In this road the lampposts were few and far between, and the driver had been careful to stop in the darkest spot he could find. He had switched headlights and sidelights off as soon as he had stopped.

Peter reached over to the front of the car and switched them on. He didn't want anything to run into his father's car and smash it. He wished he could drive, but he couldn't, and anyway, he was much too young to have a

licence. What should he do now?

Janet sat up, too, still trembling. 'Where are we?' she said. 'Have those men gone?'

'Yes. It's all right, Janet; I don't think they're coming back,' said Peter. 'Well, I wonder who they were and why they wanted to come here in the car? Talk about an adventure! We were moaning last night because there wasn't even the smell of one, and now here's one, right out of the blue!'

'Well, I don't much like an adventure in the dark,' said Janet. 'What are we going to do?'

'We must get in touch with Daddy,' said Peter. 'He must still be waiting at the station, unless he's gone home! But we haven't been more than a few minutes. I think I'll try to find a telephone box and telephone the station to see if Daddy is still there.'

'I'm not going to wait in the car by myself,' said Janet, at once. 'Oh dear, I wish we had Scamper with us. I should feel much better then.'

'The men wouldn't have taken the car if Scamper had been with us,' said Peter, getting out. 'He would have barked, and they would have run off to someone else's car. Come on, Janet, get out. I'll lock the doors in case there is anyone else who might take a fancy to Daddy's car!'

He locked all the doors, Janet holding his torch for him so that he could see what he was doing. Then they went down the street to see if they could find a telephone box anywhere.

They were lucky. One was at the corner of the very road where they were! Peter slipped inside and dialled the railway station.

'Station here,' said a voice at the other end.

'This is Peter, of Old Mill House,' said Peter. 'Is my father at the station still, by any chance?'

'Yes, he is,' said the voice. 'He's just collecting some parcels. Do you want to speak to him? Right, I'll ask him to come to the phone.'

Half a minute later Peter heard his father's voice. 'Yes? Who is it? *You*, Peter! But – but aren't you still in the car, in the station yard? Where are you?'

Peter explained everything as clearly as he could, and his father listened to his tale in amazement. 'Well! Two car thieves going off with my car and not guessing you and Janet

were in it. Where are you?'

'Janet's just asked somebody,' said Peter. 'We're in Jackson Street, not far from the Broadway. Can you get here, Dad, and fetch the car? We'll wait.'

'Yes. I'll get a taxi here in the yard,' said his father. 'Well, of all the things to happen!'

Janet and Peter went back to the car. Now that they knew their father would be along in a few minutes they no longer felt scared. Instead they began to feel rather pleased and important.

'We'll have to call a Secret Seven meeting about this *at once*,' said Peter. 'The police will be on to it, I expect, and *we'll* work on it too. What will Susie do *now*? Who cares about her silly tricks? Nobody at all!'

CHAPTER EIGHT

Another meeting

IN A short time a taxi drew up beside the car and the children's father jumped out.

'Here we are!' called Janet, as her father paid the taxi-man.

He ran over, and got into the driver's seat. 'Well! Little did I think my car had been driven away while I was in the station,' he said. 'Are you sure you're all right?'

'Oh yes,' said Peter. 'We were half asleep at the back; the men didn't even spot us. They got in and drove straight to this place, then got out. They hardly said a word to one another.'

'Oh. Well, I suppose they weren't really car thieves,' said his father. 'Just a couple of young idiots who wanted to drive somewhere instead of walk. I shan't bother to inform the police. We'd never catch the fellows, and it would be a waste of everyone's time. I've got the car back; that's all that matters.'

The two children felt a little flat to have their extraordinary adventure disposed of in this way.

'But aren't you *really* going to tell the police?' asked Peter, quite disappointed. 'The men may be real crooks.'

'They probably are. But I'm not going to waste *my* time on them,' said his father. 'They'll be caught for something sooner or later! It's a good thing you had the sense to keep quiet in the back of the car!'

Their mother was a good deal more interested in the affair than Daddy, yet even she thought it was just a silly prank on the part of two young men. But it was different when Peter telephoned Jack and told him what happened. Jack was absolutely thrilled.

'Gosh! Really! I wish I'd been with you!' he shouted in excitement, clutching the telephone hard. 'Let's have a meeting about it. Tomorrow afternoon at three o'clock? We've all got a half-term holiday tomorrow, haven't we? We'll tell the others at school there's a meeting on. I'll . . . Sh. Sh!'

'What are you shushing about?' asked Peter. 'Oh, is that awful Susie about? All right, not a word more. See you tomorrow.'

Next afternoon, at three o'clock, all the Secret Seven were down in the shed, Scamper with them too, running from one to another excitedly. He could feel that something important was afoot!

The oil-stove was already lit and the shed was nice and warm. Curtains were drawn across the windows in case anyone should peer in. Nobody had had time to bring things to eat, but fortunately George had had a present of a large bag of humbugs from his grandmother. He handed them round.

'I say, how super,' said Jack. 'Your granny does buy such ENORMOUS humbugs. They last for ages. Now we shall all be comfortable for the rest of the afternoon, with one of these in our cheeks.'

They sat round on boxes or on old rugs, each with their cheeks bulging with a peppermint humbug. Scamper didn't like them, which was lucky. The children made him sit by the door and listen in case anyone came prying, that awful Susie, for instance, or one of her silly friends!

Peter related the whole event, and everyone listened, thrilled.

'And do you mean to say your father isn't going to the police?' said Colin. 'Well, that leaves the field free for us. Come along, Secret Seven, here's something right up our street!'

'It's very exciting,' said Pam. 'But what exactly are we going to work on? I mean, what is there to find out? I wouldn't even know where to *begin*!'

'Well, I'll tell you what *I* think,' said Peter, carefully moving his humbug to the other cheek. 'I think those men are up to something. I don't know what, but I think we ought to find out something about them.'

'But how can we?' asked Pam. 'I don't like the sound of them, anyway.'

'Well, if you don't want to be in on this, there's nothing to stop you from walking out,' said Peter, getting cross with Pam. 'The door's over there.'

Pam changed her mind in a hurry. 'Oh no, I *want* to be in on this; of course I do. You tell us what to do, Peter.'

'Well we don't *know* very much,' said Peter. 'Excuse me, all of you, but I'm going to take my humbug out for a minute or two, while I talk. There, that's better. No, Scamper, don't sniff at it; you don't *like* humbugs!'

With his sweet safely on a clean piece of paper beside him, Peter addressed the meeting.

'We haven't really much to go on, as I said,' he began. 'But we have a *few* clues. One is "Sid's Place". We ought to try and find where that is and watch it, to see if either of the men go there. Then we could shadow them. We'd have to watch it at five o'clock each day.'

'Go on,' said George.

'Then there's Q8061,' said Peter. 'That might be a telephone number. We could find out about that.'

'That's silly!' said Pam. 'It doesn't look a bit like a telephone number!'

Peter took no notice of Pam. 'One man had a low-brimmed hat and long hair down to his

collar,' he said. 'And I *think* there was something wrong with one hand – it looked as if the tip of the middle finger was missing. I only *just* caught sight of it in the light of a lamppost, but I'm fairly sure.'

'And the other man had very short hair,' said Janet, suddenly. 'I did notice that. Oh, and Peter, do you remember that he said he thought he'd dropped something? Do you think he had?

We never looked to see! He didn't find what-ever it was.'

'Gosh, yes. I forgot all about that,' said Peter. 'That's most important. We'll all go and look in the car at once. Bring your torches, please, Secret Seven!'

CHAPTER NINE

The Seven get going

SCAMPER DARTED out into the garden with the Seven. Jack looked about to see if Susie or any of her friends were in hiding, but as Scamper didn't run barking at any bush, he felt sure that Susie must be somewhere else!

They all went to the garage. Peter hoped that the car would be there. It was! The children opened the doors and looked inside.

'It's no good us looking in the back,' said Peter. 'The men were in front.'

He felt about everywhere, and shone his torch into every corner of the front of the car. The garage was rather dark, although it was only half-past three in the afternoon.

'Nothing!' he said disappointed.

'Let *me* see,' said Janet. 'I once dropped a pencil and couldn't find it, and it was down between the two front seats!'

She slid her fingers in between the two seats and felt about. She gave a cry and pulled something out. It was a spectacle case. She held it up in triumph.

'Look! That's it. He dropped his spectacle case!'

'But he didn't wear glasses,' said Peter.

'He could have reading glasses, couldn't he?' said Janet. 'Like Granny?'

She opened the case. It was empty. She gave another little squeal.

'Look, it's got his name inside! What do you think of *that*? And his telephone number! *Now* we're on to something!'

The Secret Seven crossed round to look. Janet pointed to a little label inside. On it neatly written was a name and number. 'Briggs. Renning 2150.'

'Renning – that's not far away!' said Peter. 'We can look up the name in the telephone directory and see his address. Gosh, what a find!'

Everyone was thrilled. Jack was just about to shut the door of the car when he suddenly remembered that no one had looked *under* the left-hand front seat, where the man who had dropped something had sat. He took a little stick from a bundle of garden bamboos standing in a nearby corner and poked under the seat with it, and out rolled a button!

'Look!' said Jack, holding it up.

Peter gave it a glance.

'Oh that's off my father's mac,' he said. 'It must have been there for ages.'

He put it into his pocket, and they all went back to the shed, feeling very excited.

'Well, first we find out Mr Briggs' address. Then we all ride over to see him,' said Peter. 'We'll make him admit he dropped it in the car, and then I'll pounce like anything and say, "And what were you doing in my father's car?" I'm sure the police would be interested if we could actually tell them the name and address of the man who went off in Dad's car like that, and probably they would make him give the name of the other man too!'

This long speech made Peter quite out of

breath. The others gazed at him in admiration. It all sounded very bold.

'All right. What about now, this very minute, if we can find his address in Renning?' said Jack. 'Nothing like striking while the iron's hot. We could have tea in that little tea-shop in Renning. They have wonderful macaroons. I ate five last time I was there.'

'Then somebody else must have paid the bill,' said Colin. 'Yes, do let's go now. It *would* be fun, but you can do the talking, Peter!'

'Have you all got your bikes?' said Peter. 'Good. Let's just go in and take a look at the telephone directory, and get the address. Mr Briggs, we're coming after you!'

The telephone directory was very helpful. Mr H. E. J. Briggs lived at Little Hill, Raynes Road, Renning. Telephone number 2150. Peter copied it down carefully.

'Got enough money for tea, everyone?' he asked.

Colin had only a penny or two, so Peter offered to lend him some. Now they were all ready to set off.

Peter told his mother they were going out to

tea, and away they went, riding carefully in single line down the main road, as they had been taught to do.

Renning was about three miles away, and it didn't really take them long to get there.

'Shall we have tea first?' asked George, looking longingly at the tea-shop they were passing.

'No. Work first, pleasure afterwards,' said

Peter, who was always very strict about things like that. They cycled on to Raynes Road.

It was only a little lane, set with pretty little cottages. Little Hill was at one end, a nice little place with a colourful garden.

'Well it doesn't *look* like the home of a crook,' said Jack. 'But you never know. See, there's someone in the garden, Peter. Come on, do your job. Let's see how you handle things of this sort. Make him admit he dropped that spectacle case in your father's car!'

'Right!' said Peter, and went in boldly at the garden gate. 'Er – good afternoon. Are you Mr Briggs?'

CHAPTER TEN

Peter feels hot all over

As soon as Peter saw the man closely, he knew
at once that he wasn't either of the men in the
car. For one thing, this man had a big round
head, and a face to match, and both the other
men had had rather narrow heads, as far as he
had been able to see.

The man looked a little surprised. 'No,' he
said. 'I'm not Mr Briggs. I'm just a friend staying
with him. Do you want him? I'll call him?'

Peter began to feel a little uncomfortable.
Somehow this pretty garden and trim little
cottage didn't seem the kind of place those
men would live in!

'Henry! Henry, there's someone asking for
you!' called the man.

Peter saw that the other Secret Seven members were watching eagerly. Would 'Henry' prove to be one of the men they were hunting for?

A man came strolling out, someone with trim, short hair and a narrow head. Yes, he *might* be the man who had sat in the left-hand seat of the car, except that he didn't in the least look as if he could possibly take someone else's car!

Still you never know! thought Peter.

The man looked inquiringly at him. 'What do you want?' he said.

'Er – is your name Mr H. E. J. Briggs, sir?' asked Peter, politely.

'It is,' said the man looking amused. 'Why?'

'Er – well, have you by any chance lost a spectacle case?' asked Peter.

All the rest of the Seven outside the garden held their breath. What would he say?

'Yes. I *have* lost one,' said the man surprised. 'Have you found it? Where was it?'

'It was in the front of a car,' answered Peter, watching him closely.

Now if the man was one of the car-thieves, he would surely look embarrassed, or deny it.

He would know that it was the case he had dropped the night before and would be afraid of saying 'Yes, I dropped it there.'

'What an extraordinary thing!' said the man. 'Whose car? You sound rather *mysterious*. Losing a spectacle case is quite an ordinary thing to do, you know!'

'It was dropped in my father's car last night,' said Peter, still watching the man.

'Oh no, it wasn't,' said Mr Briggs at once. 'I've lost this case for about a week. It can't be mine. I wasn't in anyone's car last night.'

'It *is* the man we want, I bet it is!' said Pam in a low voice to Janet. 'He's telling fibs!'

'The case has your name in it,' said Peter, 'so we know it's yours. And it *was* in my father's car last night.'

'Who *is* your father?' said the man, sounding puzzled. 'I can't quite follow what you're getting at. And where's the case?'

'My father lives at Old Mill House,' began Peter, 'and he's . . .'

'Good gracious! He's not Jack, my farmer friend, surely?' said Mr Briggs. 'That explains everything! He very kindly gave me a lift one day last week, and I must have dropped my spectacle case in his car then. I hunted for it everywhere when I got back home. Never thought of the car, of course! Well, well, so you've brought it back?'

'Oh, are you the man my father speaks of as Harry?' said Peter, taken aback. 'Gosh! Well I suppose you *did* drop your case, then, and not last night, as I thought. Here it is. It's got your name and telephone number in it. That's how

we knew it was yours.'

He held it out, and the man took it, smiling. 'Thanks,' he said, 'and now perhaps you'll tell me what all the mystery was about, and why you insisted I had dropped it last night, and why you looked at me as if I were somebody Very Suspicious Indeed.'

Peter heard the others giggling, and he went red. He really didn't know *what* to say!

'Well,' he said, 'you see, two men took my father's car last night, and when we looked in it today we found this case, and we thought perhaps it belonged to one of the men.'

Mr Briggs laughed. 'I see, doing a little detective work. Well, it's very disappointing for you, but I don't happen to be a car-thief. Look, here's fifty pence for bringing back my case. Buy some chocolate and share it with those interested friends of yours watching over the hedge.'

'Oh no, thank you,' said Peter, backing away. 'I don't want anything. I'm only too glad to bring your case back. Goodbye!'

He went quickly out of the garden, most relieved to get away from the amused eyes of

Mr Briggs. Goodness, what a mistake! He got on his bicycle and rode swiftly away, the other six following.

They all stopped outside the tea-shop.

'Whew!' said Peter, wiping his forehead. 'I DID feel awful when I found out he was a friend of my father's! Dad is always talking about a man called Harry, but I didn't know his surname before.'

'We thought we were so clever, but we weren't this time,' said Colin. 'Bother! The spectacle case was nothing to do with those two men in the car, but perhaps the button is?'

'Perhaps,' said Peter. 'But I'm not tackling anyone wearing macs with buttons that match the one we found, unless I'm jolly certain he's one of those men! I feel hot all over when I think of Mr Briggs. Suppose he goes and tells my father all about this?'

'Never mind,' said Jack, grinning. 'It was great fun watching you. Let's have tea. Look, they've got macaroons today.'

In they went and had a wonderful tea. And now, what next? Think hard, Secret Seven, and make some exciting plans!

CHAPTER ELEVEN

Jobs for every member

THE NEXT day another Secret Seven meeting was held, but this time it was at Colin's, in his little summer-house. It wasn't such a good place as Peter's shed, because it had an open doorway with no door, and they were not allowed to have an oilstove in it.

However, Colin's mother had asked all the Secret Seven to tea, so it was clear they would have to have their next meeting at his house, and the little summer-house was the only place where they could talk in secret.

'We'll bring our old clothes for the Guy and decide what he should wear,' said Peter. 'We haven't even thought about him in the last two meetings and it's Bonfire Night in a few days.

We'll need paper and straw for stuffing him too.'

So all the Secret Seven went to Colin's house that evening. They had a fine tea, the kind they all enjoyed most.

'Sardine sandwiches, honey sandwiches, a smashing cherry cake with cherries inside *and* on top, and an iced sponge cake. I say, Colin, your mother's a wonder,' said Peter, approvingly. 'Isn't she going to have it with us? I'd like to thank her.'

'No, she's had to go out to a committee meeting or something,' said Colin. 'All she said was that we've to behave ourselves, and if we go down to the summer-house this cold dark evening, we've GOT to put on our coats.'

'Right,' said Peter. 'Coats it will be. Mothers are always very keen on coats, aren't they? Personally, I think it's quite hot today.'

They finished up absolutely everything on the tea-table. There wasn't even a piece of the big cherry cake left! Scamper, who had also been asked to tea, had his own dish of dog-biscuits with shrimp paste on each. He was simply delighted, and crunched them up nonstop.

'Now we'll go to the summer-house. We'd better take a candle it's so dark already,' said Colin. 'And don't forget your coats everyone.'

'And the things for the Guy,' said Peter.

So down they all went to the little wooden summer-house, carrying paper, straw, string and safety pins as well as an odd assortment of old clothes. The house had a wooden bench running all round it and felt a bit cold. Nobody minded that. It was such a nice secret place to talk in, down at the bottom of the dark garden.

The candle was stuck in a bottle and lit. There was no shelf to put it on, so Colin stood it in the middle of the floor.

'Have to be careful of Scamper knocking it over!' said Peter. 'Where is he?'

'He's gone into the kitchen to see Daddy,' said Colin. 'He's cooking a stew or something, and Scamper smelt it. He'll be along soon. Now stack your things under the wooden bench for the time being. That's right. We'll look at the clothes when we've finished the meeting.'

'We'll begin it now,' said Peter. 'Owing to our

silly mistake about the spectacles case, we're not as far on with this adventure as we ought to be. We must do a little more work on it. First, has anyone any idea where "Sid's place" is?'

There was a silence.

'Never heard of it,' said Jack.

'Well, it must be some place that is used by men like those two in my father's car,' said Peter.

'Perhaps Larry at the garage would know?' said Colin, who had great faith in Larry. 'He knows a lot of lorry-drivers, and they're the kind who might go to some place called "Sid's" or "Jim's" or "Nick's".'

'Yes. That's a good idea,' said Peter. 'Colin, you and George go and find out from Larry tomorrow. Now, what else can we do? What about the number that one of the men had to get in touch with – what was it now?'

'Q8061,' said Pam, promptly. 'I think of it as the *letter* Q, but it might be spelt K-E-W, you know.'

'Yes, you're right. It might,' said Peter. 'That's really quite an idea, Pam. It might be a telephone number at Kew telephone exchange, Kew 8061. You and Barbara can make it your job to find out.'

'How do we set about it?' said Barbara.

'I really can't explain such easy things to you,' said Peter, impatiently. 'You and Pam can quite well work out what to do yourselves. Now is there anything else we can work on?'

'Only the button we found in the car,' said Jack.

'I told you, it's sure to belong to my father's mac,' said Peter. 'It's just like the buttons on it.'

'But we ought to make *sure*,' argued Jack. 'You know you always say we never ought to leave anything to chance, Peter. There are hundreds of different coat buttons.'

'Well, perhaps you're right,' said Peter. 'Yes, I think you are. Janet, will you see to that point, please, and look at Dad's mac. I know he's got a button missing, so I expect it belongs to his mac, but we *will* make sure.'

'You haven't given *me* anything to do,' said Jack.

'Well, if the button doesn't match the ones on Dad's mac, you can take charge of *that* point,' said Peter, with a sudden giggle, 'and you can march about looking for people wearing a mac with a missing button.'

'Don't be an idiot,' said Jack. 'Still, if it *isn't* your father's button, it *will* be one dropped by one of those men, and one of us ought to take charge of it. So I will, if it's necessary.'

'Right,' said Peter. 'Well, that's the end of the meeting. Now let's think about the Guy.'

CHAPTER TWELVE

Oh, what a pity!

COLIN AND Jack took the bundles of clothes for the Guy out from under the wooden bench of the summer-house. The Seven knelt down on the floor to sort everything out. What a lovely job!

'I wish we had a better light than just this flickering candle on the floor,' said Pam. 'It's difficult to see what colour the clothes are.'

Colin pulled out a fearsome-looking mask from the pile of old things. 'Who brought this? It looks like the villain in that play we saw on TV last night. He put on the mask and hissed menacingly, "Your money or your life."'

'You look worse than that villain, Colin,' said Janet. 'I got the mask at a party ages ago and I put it away for Guy Fawkes. I almost forgot where I had put it.'

'It will make a really frightening Guy. I can just imagine him leering down at us from the top of the bonfire,' said Barbara.

'We'd better start making the Guy,' said Peter. 'This is a good big pair of trousers. If we stuff straw and screwed up paper down the legs we can safety pin those old slippers on the bottoms to look like feet.'

'And here's your father's old green jacket, George. We can do the same to the arms and pin my old gloves on for hands,' said Barbara, 'though his hands will look a bit smaller than the rest of him!'

'Look what I've brought,' said Pam. 'I thought it would be much easier to have an old cushion for a body instead of straw and paper. Mother said I could take this old blue one that has been leaking stuffing.'

The Secret Seven began to roll up paper and stuff straw into the trousers and jacket. It was difficult to see what they were doing with only the light of the candle. As they worked, they heard the sound of a bark, and then scampering feet. Scamper had been let out of the kitchen door and was coming to find his friends. Where were they? Wuff! Wuff!

'Scamper!' called Janet from the summer-house. 'We're here!'

Scamper tore down the garden path, barking madly. Anyone would think he had been away from the seven children for a whole month, not just half an hour!

He rushed straight into the little summer-house and over went the bottle with the lit candle in its neck! Crash!

'You idiot, Scamper,' said Peter and reached to set the bottle upright again. The candle was still alight.

But before he could take hold of it, the flame

of the candle had licked against a bundle of straw. It was alight!

'Fire!' yelled Peter. 'Look out, Pam! Look out, Barbara!'

The straw flared up and the loose paper on the floor began to burn too. The children tried to stamp out the flames but the fire spread faster than they could stamp.

Flames licked at the wooden bench. The old clothes were smouldering, sending out black smoke that made the children cough and splutter.

The seven children hurried out of the little summer-house clutching each other. Scamper, really terrified, had completely disappeared.

They all turned to look back. Fire glowed through the doorway and windows. They could hear a crackling as their things burned.

'We'd better get some water,' said Colin, suddenly. 'The summer-house will catch fire and burn down. Quick!'

They left the fire and ran to get buckets. There was a little pond nearby, and they filled the buckets from it. Splash! Splash! Splash! The water was thrown all over the summer-house, and there was a tremendous sizzling

noise. Black smoke poured out of the little house and almost choked the Seven.

'Pooh!' said Jack, and coughed. 'What a horrible smell!'

'It's a good thing your father didn't see this,' panted Peter to Colin, coming up with another pail of water. 'He would be furious about this. There, I think we've about got the fire down now. POOOOOH! That smoke!'

It was a very, very sad ending to the tea and meeting at Colin's. Barbara was in tears. There was nothing left of the Guy but smoke and smell and a nasty-looking black mess.

'It's bad luck,' said Peter, feeling as if he wouldn't mind howling himself. 'Bother Scamper! It's all his fault. Where is he?'

'Gone home at sixty miles an hour, I should think,' said Janet. 'It's a pity he hasn't got a post-office savings book like we have. I'd make him take some money out and buy another mask for us.'

'We'll have to see if we can collect some more clothes. But I don't suppose people will want to give us any more after this,' said George.

'I hope your parents won't be too cross

about the summer-house,' said Jack gloomily. 'At least it didn't burn down, but everything is very black and wet. The wooden bench is a bit charred too. I'll come along tomorrow, when it's dried up a bit, and help you to clear it up.'

They were just about to go off to the front gate when Janet stopped them. 'We meant to choose a new password today,' she said. 'You know that Susie knows our last one, "Guy Fawkes", and we really *must* have a secret one. Susie has told everyone in our class.'

'Yes. I forgot about that,' said Peter. 'Well, I vote we have "Bonfire". It really does seem a very good password for tonight!'

'All right – Bonfire,' said Colin. 'I'm sorry it's been such a disappointing evening. This is definitely *not* the kind of adventure I like! Goodbye, all of you. See you tomorrow!'

It was a gloomy company of children that made their way home. Bother Scamper, *why* did he have to do a silly thing like that?

CHAPTER THIRTEEN

Sid's Place

ALL THE Secret Seven felt exceedingly gloomy next day, which was Sunday. They met at Sunday School, but none of them had much to say. They were all very subdued. Colin's parents had been very cross about the damaged summer-house and had forbidden him ever to use candles there again.

'Scamper *did* race home last night,' said Janet to the girls. 'He was behind the couch, trembling from head to foot. He is awfully frightened of fire you know.'

'Poor Scamper!' said Pam. 'Did you forgive him?'

'We simply had to,' said Janet. 'Anyway, he didn't mean to upset the candle, poor Scamper. We stroked him and patted him and loved him, and when he saw we weren't going to scold him, he crept out and sat as close to our legs as he could, and put his head on my knee.'

'He's so sweet,' said Barbara. 'But all the same it's *dreadful* to have lost our Guy.'

'It's quite put our adventure out of my mind,' said Pam. 'But I suppose we'd better think about it again tomorrow, Barbara. We've got to find out about that telephone number, Kew 8061. Though how we shall do it, I don't know.'

'Leave it till tomorrow,' said Barbara. 'I can't think of anything but our poor Guy today.'

The next day was Monday, and the Seven were back at school. George and Colin went to call at the garage after morning school, to try and find out something about 'Sid's Place' from Larry. He was sitting in a corner with a newspaper, munching his lunch.

'Hallo, Larry,' said Colin. 'I wonder if you can help us. Do you know anywhere called "Sid's Place"?'

'No, I don't,' said Larry. 'Sounds like an eating-house or something. There's a lorry-driver coming in soon. If you like to wait, I'll ask him.'

The lorry drove in after three or four minutes, and the man got down, a big heavy fellow who called out cheerfully to Larry. 'Just off to get a bite of dinner. Be back in half an hour for my lorry.'

'Hey, Charlie, do you eat at "Sid's Place"?' called Larry. 'Do you know it?'

'"Sid's Place"? No, I eat at my sister's when I come through here,' said Charlie. 'Wait a minute now. "Sid's" you said. Yes I remember seeing a little café called "Sid's Café". Would that be the place you're meaning?'

'Could be,' said Larry, looking questioningly at Colin.

Colin nodded. 'Probably the one,' he said, feeling suddenly excited. 'Where is it?'

'You know Old Street? Well, it's at the corner of Old Street and James Street, not a first-class place, and not the sort you boys want to go to. So long, Larry. See you in half an hour!'

'Thanks, Larry,' said Colin. 'Come on, George, let's go and have a look at this place. We've just about got time.'

They went to Old Street and walked down to James Street at the end. On the corner, sharing a bit of each street, was a rather dirty-looking eating-house. 'Sid's Café' was painted over the top of the very messy window.

The boys looked inside. Men were sitting at a long counter, eating sandwiches and drinking coffee or tea. There were one or two tables in the shop, too, at which slightly better-dressed men were having a hot meal served to them by a fat and cheerful girl.

'Oh so that's "Sid's Place",' said Colin, staring in. 'I wonder which is Sid?'

'Perhaps Sid is somewhere in the back quarters,' said George. 'There are only girls serving here. Well we know that one of those men comes here every day about five o'clock. One of us must watch, and we'll be bound to see the man.'

'It'll have to be Peter,' said Colin. 'We wouldn't know the man. He would probably recognise him at once.'

'Yes. It's going to be very difficult for him to hang about here, watching everyone,' said George. 'People will wonder what he's up to. Two of us would seem even *more* suspicious.'

'Well that's up to Peter!' said Colin. 'We've done *our* job and found Sid's place. Come on, we'll be awfully late for lunch.'

Peter was very pleased with Colin and George when he heard their news. 'Good work!' he said. 'I'll get along there at five o'clock this afternoon. How have Pam and Barbara got on?'

Janet told him while they had a quick tea together after afternoon school. 'They just couldn't think *how* to do anything about KEW 8061,' said Janet. 'They simply couldn't.'

'Couple of idiots!' said Peter, munching a bun quickly. 'Hurry up, I must go.'

'Well, Pam asked her mother how to find out if there *was* such a number, because she and Barbara really didn't feel they could wade all through the telephone directories,' said Janet. 'And her mother said, "Well, just ring up and see if there's an answer!"'

'Easy,' said Peter. 'Simple!'

'Yes – well, they rang up the number, feeling very excited, because they thought they could ask whoever answered what his name and address were, but there was no reply,' said Janet. 'And the operator said it was because there was no telephone with that number at present! So Q8061 is *not* a telephone number, Peter. It must be something else!'

'Bother!' said Peter, getting up. 'It would have been marvellous if KEW 8061 *had* answered. We'd have been able to get the name and address and everything. That clue isn't much good, I'm afraid. I must be off, Janet. Wouldn't it be wonderful if I spotted one of the men going into Sid's place?'

'It *would*,' said Janet. 'Oh, I DO hope you do, Peter!'

CHAPTER FOURTEEN

A wonderful idea

PETER WENT as quickly as he could to the corner of Old Street and James Street. Yes – there was Sid's Café, just as Colin had said. What was the time?

He glanced at his watch – six minutes to five. Well, if the man came at five o'clock, he ought just to catch him. Of course, he might come any time after that. That would be a nuisance, because then Peter would have to wait about a long time.

Peter lolled against the corner, watching everyone who came by, especially, of course, the men who went in and out of 'Sid's Café'. They were mostly men with barrows of fruit that they left outside, or drivers of

vans, or shifty-looking men, unshaved and dirty.

He got a shock when someone came out of the café and spoke roughly to him.

'Now then, what are you doing here, lolling about? Don't you dare take fruit off my barrow! I've caught you boys doing it before, and I'll call the police if you do. Clear off!'

'I wouldn't *dream* of taking your fruit!' said Peter, indignantly, looking at the pile of cheap fruit on the nearby barrow.

'Ho, you wouldn't, would you? Well, then,

what are you standing here for, looking about? Boys don't stand at corners for nothing! We've been watching you from inside the shop, me and my mates, and we know you're after something!'

Peter was shocked. How dare this man say things like that to him! Still, perhaps some boys did steal from barrows or from fruit-stalls outside shops.

'Go on, you tell me what you're standing about here for,' said the man again, putting his face close to Peter's.

As the boy couldn't tell him the reason why he was standing at that corner, he said nothing, but turned and went off, his face burning red. Horrible man! he thought. And I haven't seen anyone yet in the least like that man who went off in our car. Of course, all I've got to go on really is his hat and long hair, and possibly maimed finger on his right hand.

He ran back home, thinking hard. After all, that man might go to Sid's place each night and I'd *never* know him if he had a cap instead of a hat, and had cut his hair shorter. And most of these men slouch along with their hands in their pockets, so I wouldn't see his hand either. It's hopeless.

Peter went round to see Colin about it. Jack and George were there, doing their homework together.

'Hallo!' they said, in surprise. 'Aren't you watching at Sid's place?'

Peter told them what had happened. 'I don't see how I can go and watch there any more,' he said, rather gloomily. 'That man who spoke to me was really nasty. And how can I watch without being seen?'

'Can't be done,' said Colin. 'Give it up! This is something we just can't do. Come on out to the summer-house and see what I've made! We cleared away the mess from the fire, and I've got something else there now!'

They all went out to the summer-house, with their torches. Colin shone his on to something there, and Peter jumped in astonishment, not at first realising what it was.

'Gosh! It's a Guy!' he said, in admiration. 'What a beauty!'

The Guy certainly was very fine. He was stuffed with straw, and wore some of Colin's

very old clothes. He had a mask, of course, and grinned happily at the three boys. He had a wig made of black strands of wool and an old hat on top. Colin had sat him in a garden barrow, and he really looked marvellous.

'He's not man-sized because I only had my very old and small suit, but he's the best I could do,' said Colin. 'I bought another mask with my pocket money. Dad said we can have a bonfire at the bottom of the garden as long as he is there. You can all come and help build it tomorrow.'

The Guy seemed to watch them as they talked, grinning away merrily.

'It's a pity *he* can't watch outside Sid's place!' said Jack. 'Nobody would suspect him or bother about *him*. He could watch for that fellow all evening!'

They all laughed. Then Peter stopped suddenly and gazed hard at the Guy. An idea had come to him, a really WONDERFUL idea!

'Hey!' he said, clutching at Colin and making him jump. 'You've given me an idea! What about ME dressing up as a Guy, and wearing a mask with eye-holes – and one of you taking me somewhere near Sid's Café? There are heaps of these Guys about now, and nobody would think our Guy was *real*. I would watch for ages and nobody would guess.'

'Whew!' said the other three together, and stared at Peter in admiration.

Colin thumped him on the back. 'That's a brilliant idea!' he said. 'Super! Smashing! When shall we do it?'

'Tomorrow,' said Peter. 'I can rush here and dress up easily enough, and one of you can wheel me off in the barrow – all of you, if you like! What a game!'

'But my mother doesn't like the idea of children taking Guys and begging for money,' said Colin, remembering. 'She says that begging is wrong.'

'So it is,' said Peter. 'My mother says that too, but if we *did* get any money we could give it to a charity.'

'Oh well, that's all right, then!' said Colin. 'Gosh, this is grand! Mind you don't leap up out of the barrow if you see that fellow going into Sid's place, Peter!'

'I'll keep as still as a real Guy!' said Peter, grinning. 'Well, so long. See you at school tomorrow.'

CHAPTER FIFTEEN

The peculiar Guy

PETER RACED home to tell Janet of the new idea. She was so thrilled that she couldn't say a word. What an idea! How super! She stared in admiration at her brother. He was truly a fine leader for the Secret Seven!

Scamper wuffed loudly, exactly as if he were saying, 'Great, Peter, splendid idea!'

'*I've* got something to tell you, too,' said Janet, suddenly remembering. 'I looked on Daddy's mac and he *has* got a button missing; but it's a small one on his sleeve, not a large one like we found. And also it's not quite the same colour, Peter.'

'Ah, good! That means it probably *was* a button that dropped from that man's mac!'

said Peter, pleased. 'Jack will have to take the button, Janet, and work on that clue, if he can! So give it to me, and I'll hand it to him tomorrow.'

'I wish we could find out about Q8061,' said Janet. 'I'm pretty sure it must be someone's telephone number, but it's very difficult to find out.'

'There's Mother calling,' said Peter. 'I bet it's to tell me to do my homework!'

It was of course, and poor Peter found it very difficult indeed to work out arithmetic problems when his head was full of dressing up as a Guy!

All the Secret Seven were thrilled to hear of Peter's new plan, and next evening they were round at Colin's to see him dress up. He really did look remarkably good!

He wore an old pair of patched trousers, and a ragged jacket. He wore a pair of great big boots thrown out by Colin's father. He had a scarf round his neck, and a big old hat over a wig made of black wool.

'You look quite *dreadful*!' said Janet, with a giggle. 'Put the mask on now.'

Peter put it on, and immediately became a grinning Guy, like all the other Guys that were appearing here and there in the streets of the town. Scamper took one look at Peter's suddenly changed face, and backed away, growling.

'It's all right, Scamper,' said Peter, laughing. 'It's me! Don't be afraid.'

'You look horrible,' said Pam. 'I really feel scared when I look at you, though I know you're really Peter. Nobody, *nobody* could possibly guess you were alive!'

Peter got into the barrow. 'Gosh, it's very

hard and uncomfortable,' he said. 'Got any old cushions, Colin?'

Colin produced an old rug and three rather dirty garden cushions. These made the barrow much more comfortable. Peter got in and lolled on the cushions in the limp, floppy way of all Guys. He really looked extremely Guy-like!

The others shrieked with laughter to see him.

'Come on,' said Colin at last. 'We really must go, or we shan't be there till long past five.'

The three boys set off, taking turns at wheeling Peter in the barrow. He kept making horrible groans and moans, and Jack laughed so much that he had to sit down on a bus-stop seat and hold his aching sides.

An old lady there peered at the Guy. 'What a good one!' she said, and fumbled in her purse. 'I'll give you some money for fireworks.'

'Oh, any money we get is going to charity,' explained George quickly.

She gave him fifty pence, and then, as the bus came up, waved to them and got on.

'How nice of her!' said George. 'Fifty whole pence.'

They went on down the street, with Peter

thoroughly enjoying himself! He lolled about, watching everything through the eye-slits of his mask, and made silly remarks in a hollow Guy-like voice that made the others laugh helplessly.

At last they came to Sid's Café. The barrow was neatly wedged into a little alcove near the door, from which Peter could see everyone who went in or out.

The boys stood nearby, waiting to see if Peter recognised anyone. If he did, he was to give a sign, and two of the Seven would shadow the man to see where he went, if he happened to come *out* of the café. If he went inside it they were to wait till he came out.

The men going in and out of the eating-house were amused with the Guy. One prodded him hard with his stick, and gave Peter a terrible shock. 'Good Guy you've got there!' said the man and threw five pence on to Peter's tummy.

'Colin! Jack! You're NOT to let people prod me like that,' said Peter, in a fierce whisper. 'It really hurt.'

'Well, how are we to stop them?' said Colin, also in a whisper.

All went well till two young men came by and saw the Guy sitting there. 'Hallo! He's a good Guy!' said one. 'Nice pair of boots he's got. I've a good mind to take them off him!'

And to Peter's horror, he felt the boots on his feet being tugged hard. He gave a yell, and the young men looked extremely startled. They disappeared quickly.

'CAN'T you look after me better?' said Peter to the others. 'Heave me up a bit on the cushions. Those men pulled me off.'

Colin and George heaved him into a more comfortable position.

'Anyway, you've made quite a bit of money,' said George, in Peter's ear. 'People think you're jolly good, we've got quite a few pounds.'

Peter grunted. He was cross with the others. Why didn't they guard him from pokes and prods and pullings? Then, quite suddenly, he caught sight of somebody, and stiffened all over.

Surely, SURELY, that was one of the men who had taken his father's car? Peter stared and stared. Was it? Oh, why didn't he stand a bit nearer so that he could see?

CHAPTER SIXTEEN

The two men

THE MAN was standing by the window of the café, as if he were waiting for someone. He had on a hat and his hair was rather long. Peter looked as closely at him as he could.

The man who drove the car had a low-brimmed hat, he thought and long hair. This man somehow *looks* like that man we saw in the car.

The man moved a little nearer, and coughed impatiently. He took a handkerchief from his pocket and blew his nose loudly. The top of one middle finger was missing. Peter knew for *certain* that it was the man he was looking for! It *must* be the man! Perhaps he's waiting for the other man.

Almost before he had finished thinking this,

the second man came up! There was no mistaking that cap and the short, cropped hair, grown a little longer now. The cap was pulled down over his face exactly as it had been when he was in the car. He wore an old mac, and Peter tried to see if it had a button missing.

The two men said a word of greeting and then went into the café. They went right through the room to a door at the back, opened it, and disappeared.

'Colin! George! Jack! Those were the two men,' called Peter in a low voice full of excitement. 'One of them had half a finger missing. I saw it.'

'And the other had a button off his mac!' said Jack. 'I noticed that, though I didn't know he was one of the men we're after! But seeing that I'm in charge of the button now, I'm making a point of looking carefully at every mac I see! I believe our button matches his exactly.'

'Good work!' said Peter. 'Now listen. The next move is very, very important. Two of you must shadow these men. If they separate, you must separate too, and each go after one of them. Colin, you must wheel me home.'

'Right,' said the three, always willing to obey Peter's leadership. He really was very good at this kind of thing.

'Get as close to those men as you can and see

if you can hear anything useful,' said Peter. 'And track them right to their homes if you can. Report to me at the Secret Seven shed as soon as you can.'

'Right,' said George and Jack, feeling as if they were first-class plain-clothes policemen!

The two men were not long in Sid's. They came out after about ten minutes, looking angry. They stood in the doorway, taking no notice of the Guy and the boys.

'Sid's let us down,' said the man with the

missing finger. 'He said he'd give us two hundred and now he's knocked it down to fifty. Better go back to Q's and tell him. He'll be wild.'

The boys listened intently, pretending to fiddle about with the Guy.

'I'm not arguing with Sid again,' said the other man. 'I reckon I'm an idiot to come out of hiding, yet, till my hair's grown. Come on, let's go.'

They went off down the street, and George and Jack immediately set off behind them, leaving Colin with Peter.

'Did you hear that?' said Peter, in great excitement, forgetting he was a Guy. 'They've stolen something and want to sell it to Sid, and he won't give them what he promised. So they're going back to Q, whoever he is, probably the chief, to report it. Well we know that Q is a man, now!'

'And did you hear what the other man said about his hair growing?' said Colin, bending over Peter. 'I bet he's just come out of prison, it's so short. They always shave it there, don't they? Or perhaps he's an *escaped* prisoner, in hiding. Gosh, Peter, this is super!'

THE TWO MEN

'Wheel me to our shed,' commanded Peter, wishing he could get out and walk. 'Hurry up. The girls will be there already, and George and Jack will join us as soon as they can. Do hurry up! ... I'm going to get out and walk,' announced Peter. 'It's a nice dark road we're in. Stop a minute, Colin, and I'll get out.'

Colin stopped, and Peter climbed out of the barrow. Colin shone his torch to help him, and an old man with a dog saw the Guy stepping out of the barrow. He stared as if he couldn't believe his eyes, and then hurried off at top speed. Good gracious! A Guy coming alive. No, surely his eyes must have deceived him!

It wasn't long before Colin and Peter were whispering the password outside the shed at the bottom of Peter's garden. The barrow was shoved into some bushes, and Peter had taken off his mask.

'Bonfire!' said the boys, and the door opened at once. Pam gave a little scream as Peter came in, still looking very peculiar with a black wool wig, an old hat, and very ragged clothes.

'We've got news!' said Peter. 'Great news. Just listen, all of you!'

CHAPTER SEVENTEEN

Good work!

PETER QUICKLY told the girls all that had happened, and they listened in silence, feeling very thrilled. Now they were really finding out something, and even that button had helped!

'I think the short-haired man has either just come out of prison or escaped from it,' said Peter. 'He may have committed a robbery before he went in, and have hidden what he stole, and it's these goods he and the other man are trying to sell to Sid.'

'Well, who's Q, then?' asked Janet. 'Where does *he* come in?'

'He's probably holding the stolen goods,' said Peter, working everything out in his mind. 'And I expect he's sheltering the thief, too. If only we could find out who Q is and where he lives. He's the missing link.'

The five of them talked and talked, and Scamper listened and joined in with a few wuffs now and again, thumping his tail on the ground when the chatter got very loud.

'When will George and Jack be back?' asked Pam. 'I ought not to be too late home, and it's a quarter past six now!'

'Here they are!' said Colin, hearing voices outside. A knock came at the door.

'Password!' shouted everyone.

'Bonfire!' said two voices, and in went George and Jack, beaming all over their faces, glad to be out of the cold, dark November night.

'What happened? Did you shadow them?' demanded Peter, as they sat down on boxes.

'Yes,' said George. 'We followed them all the way down the street, and away by the canal and up by Cole Square. We only once got near enough to hear them say anything.'

'What was that?' asked Peter.

'One of them said "Is that a policeman lying in wait for us over there? Come on, run for it!"' said George. 'And just as a bobby came out of the shadows they ran round the corner, and the policeman never even noticed them! We shot after them, just in time to see them trying the handles of some cars parked there.'

'Then they slid quickly into one and drove off,' finished Jack. 'That was the end of our shadowing.'

'So they stole *another* car!' said Colin.

GOOD WORK!

'You didn't take the number by any chance, did you?' asked Peter.

'Of course!' said Jack, and took out his notebook. 'Here it is, PLK 100. We didn't go back and tell the policeman. We thought we'd race back here and let you decide what we ought to do next.'

'Good work,' said Peter, pleased. 'If only we knew where Q lived, we'd know where the men were, and could tell the police to go and grab them there. They'd get the stolen goods too. I bet they're being held by our mysterious Q!'

'I know! I know!' suddenly yelled Pam, making everyone jump. 'Why can't we look up all the names beginning with Q in our local telephone directory? If Q lives somewhere here, his name would be there, and his number.'

'Yes but there might be a lot of Qs, and we wouldn't know which was the right one,' objected Janet. 'Why, we ourselves know a Mrs Queen, a Mr Quigley and a Miss Quorn.'

'But don't you see what I *mean*!' said Pam, impatiently. 'We'll go down all the list of Qs, and the one with the telephone number of 8061 will be *our* Q! Don't you *see*?'

Everyone saw what she meant at once.

Peter looked at Pam admiringly. 'That's a very good idea, Pam,' he said. 'I've sometimes thought that you're not as good a Secret Seven member as the others are, but now I know you are. That's a Very Good Idea. Why didn't we think of it before instead of messing about with K.E.W.?'

'I'll get our telephone directory with all the numbers in,' said Janet and raced off.

She soon came back, gave the password and joined the others. She opened the book at the Qs, and everyone craned to look at them.

There were not very many. 'Quant,' read Pam, 'telephone number 6015. Queen, 6453, Quelling, 4322, Quentin, 8061 . . .! That's it. Look, here it is, Quentin, 8061, Barr's Warehouse East End. Why, that's only about two miles away, right at the other end of the town.'

'Gosh!' said Peter, delighted. 'That's given us JUST the information we wanted. A warehouse, too. A fine place for hiding stolen goods! My goodness, we've done some excellent work. Pam, you deserve a pat on the back!'

She got plenty of pats, and sat back, beaming. 'What do we do now?' she said.

GOOD WORK!

Before anyone could answer, there came the sound of footsteps down the path, and Peter's mother's voice called loudly: 'Peter! Janet! Are Colin and George there, and Pam? Their mothers have just telephoned to say they really must come home at once, it's getting late!'

'Right, Mummy!' called Peter. 'Wait for us. We've got a wonderful tale to tell you! Do wait!'

But his mother had gone scurrying back to the house, not liking the cold, damp evening. The seven children tore after her, with Scamper barking his head off.

Just as they went in at the back of the house, there came a knock at the front door.

'See who that is, Peter!' called his mother. 'I've got a cake in the oven I must look at.'

Peter went to the door, with the others close behind him. A big policeman stood there. He smiled at the surprised children.

'I've just been to Jack's house,' he said, 'and Susie told me he might be here. I saw you tonight in Cole Square – you and this other boy here. Well, not long after that somebody reported to me that their car had been stolen

near where you were, and I wondered if either of you had noticed anything suspicious going on.'

'Oh, come in, come in!' cried Peter, joyfully. 'We can tell you a whole lot about the thieves, and we can even tell you where you'll probably find the car. Come in, do!'

CHAPTER EIGHTEEN

Don't worry, Secret Seven!

THE POLICEMAN went into the hall, looking extremely surprised. Peter's mother came from the kitchen and Peter's father looked out of his study.

'What's all this?' he said. 'Nobody has got into trouble, surely?'

'No,' said Peter. 'Oh, Daddy, you must just listen to our tale. It's really super!'

They all went into the study, the policeman looking more and more puzzled.

'I *think* you'll find that stolen car outside Barr's Warehouse, at the East End of the town,' said Peter. 'And in the warehouse you'll probably find a Mr Quentin, and quite a lot of stolen goods on the premises.'

115

'And you'll find a man with half a finger missing, and another whose hair is so short that he looks like an escaped prisoner,' put in Colin.

'Wait! Wait a minute! What's this about a man with a missing half-finger?' said the policeman, urgently. 'We're looking for him – Fingers, he's called, and he's a friend of a thief who's just been in prison. He escaped last week, and we thought he might go to Fingers for help, so we've been keeping an eye open for him too.'

'They met at Sid's Café,' said Peter, enjoying everyone's astonishment.

'WHAT?' said his father. 'Sid's Café? That horrible place! Don't dare to tell me you boys have been in there.'

'Not inside, only outside,' said Peter. 'It's all right, Daddy. We *really* haven't done anything wrong. It all began with that night when you left Janet and me in your car in the station yard, and two men got in and drove it away.'

'And we wanted you to go to the police, but

you didn't think you'd bother,' said Janet. 'So we've been trying to trace the two men ourselves, and we have!'

Then the whole of the story came out how they found Sid's Café, how Peter dressed up as a Guy to watch for the men, how they saw Fingers with his missing half-finger, and how George and Jack followed them and saw them steal the car near Cole Square.

'And we know where they've gone, because they have a friend called Q, a Mr Quentin,' said Peter. 'They mentioned his telephone number, it was 8061, and we looked up the number and found the address. We only did that a little while ago, actually. The address is Barr's Warehouse, as we said.'

'Amazing!' said the policeman, scribbling fast in his notebook. 'Incredible! Do these kids do this kind of thing often?'

'Well, you're a fairly new man here,' said Peter's father, 'or you'd know how they keep poking their noses into all sorts of things. I don't know that I really approve of it, but they certainly have done some good work.'

'We're the Secret Seven Society, you see,'

explained Janet. 'And we really do like some kind of adventurous job to do.'

'Well, thanks very much,' said the policeman, getting up. 'I'll get a few men and ask the Sergeant to come along with us and see what we can find in Barr's Warehouse. You'll deserve a jolly good Bonfire Night tomorrow! I hope you've got a wonderful collection of fireworks, you deserve the best!'

'Our families are joining together for a big bonfire party. We all saved up for the fireworks and Colin's father is keeping them for us – though I expect all our fathers will take turns letting them off!'

'Well, have a good evening then – and mind you all take care not to get too close!' said the policeman, going to the door. 'I'm much obliged to you all. Good night!'

'What a tale!' said Peter's mother. 'I never heard of such goings-on! Whatever will you Seven do next? To think of you dressing up as a Guy, Peter, and watching outside Sid's Café! No wonder you look so DREADFUL! Take that black wig off, do!'

'Mummy, *can't* the others stay and have a bit

of supper?' begged Peter. 'We've got such a lot to talk about. Do let them. Sandwiches will do. We'll all help to make them.'

'Very well,' said his mother, laughing at all the excited faces. 'Janet, go and telephone everybody's mothers and tell them where they are!'

The Seven were very pleased. In fifteen minutes' time they were all sitting down to potted meat sandwiches, oatmeal biscuits, apples and hot cocoa, talking nineteen to the dozen, with a very excited Scamper tearing round their legs under the table. What an unexpected party! thought Scamper, delighted, and what a wonderful selection of titbits!

The telephone suddenly rang, and Peter went

to answer it. It proved to be a very exciting call indeed! He came racing back to the others.

'That was that policeman! He thought we'd like to know what happened.'

'What? Tell us!' cried everyone.

'Well, the police went to Barr's Warehouse and the first thing they saw in the yard was the stolen car!' said Peter. 'Then they forced their way in at the back door, and found Mr Quentin, scared stiff, in his office. When they told him they knew that Fingers and the escaped prisoner were somewhere in the warehouse, he just crumpled up!'

'Have they got the others?' asked Colin.

'Oh yes. Quentin showed the police where they were hiding,' said Peter. 'Down in a cellar, and the stolen goods were there too. It was a wonderful raid! By the way, the police want to know if we can identify the second man, the close-cropped man, and I said yes, if he was wearing a mac with a missing button, because we've got the button!'

'Goody, goody!' said Barbara. 'So we have. We forgot to tell the policeman about that! Where *is* the button?'

'Here,' said Jack, and spun it on the table. 'Good old button, you did your bit too! Gosh, this is one of the most exciting jobs the Secret Seven have ever done. I'm jolly sorry it's ended.'

So was everyone. They didn't want that exciting evening to come to a finish, but they had to say goodbye at last.

'Tomorrow is Bonfire Night,' said Peter to Janet as they shut the front door on the others. 'We'll all have a wonderful party and Colin's Guy will look down on us all from the top of the bonfire.'

'Shall we put you there instead, Peter? You'd look even better!' said Janet, smiling.

'I'd much rather watch the Guy than be him tomorrow night,' said Peter, 'though it was exciting being a Guy just for one night! Come on, Janet, let's go up to bed and dream about all those super fireworks – '

They both ran upstairs shouting at the tops of their voices, 'Bang! Whoosh! Bang-Bang-Bang!'